The Fox and the Stork

Written by Simon Puttock
Illustrated by Milly Teggle

Collins

2

4

6

10

And she did!

Fox's trick

Stork's trick

Ideas for reading

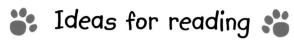

Written by Clare Dowdall, PhD
Lecturer and Primary Literacy Consultant

Learning objectives: children read and understand simple sentences; they answer 'how' and 'why' questions in response to stories; they talk about their own and others' behaviour, and its consequences, and know that some behaviour is unacceptable

Curriculum links: Personal, social and emotional development: Managing feelings and behaviour

High frequency words: the, and, come, me, on, she

Interest words: fox, stork, dine, I'll, trick, tee hee, yum

Resources: sticky notes, the internet, stories about foxes

Word count: 32

Getting started

- Look at the front cover together and discuss the two animals in the picture. Explain that the bird is called a stork. Ask children what they know about foxes in stories, and what they notice about the stork. Encourage children to decide whether they think the fox and stork are friends.

- Read the blurb aloud, pointing to each word as you read it. Ask children to explain what a trick is, and to tell stories about tricks that they have played on people.

- Look at the word *tricks*. Ask children to practise reading the word fluently and discuss what the word means.

Reading and responding

- Turn to pp2–3. Model how to read the words in the speech bubble, using a sly voice for the fox. Introduce the term *speech bubble*.

- Look at the word *dine* closely. Ask children to suggest what it means. Encourage them to use the pictures to gain some clues about the meaning of the word.